AUG   2012

MAKE YOUR OWN

ACTION THRILLER

by Jonathan Quijano

Consultant:
Tad Kershner
Founder
Montalto Visual

Velocity is published by Capstone Press,
1710 Roe Crest Drive, North Mankato, Minnesota 56003.
www.capstonepub.com

 Books published by Capstone Press are manufactured with paper
containing at least 10 percent post-consumer waste.

Library of Congress Cataloging-in-Publication Data
Quijano, Jonathan.
Make your own action thriller / Jonathan Quijano.
  p. cm.—(Velocity: make your movie)
Summary: "Provides instructions for how to make your own action-thriller movie"—Provided by
publisher.
Includes bibliographical references and index.
Includes webliography.
ISBN 978-1-4296-7529-1 (library binding)
1. Action and adventure films—Production and direction—Juvenile literature. I. Title. II. Series.
PN1995.9.A3Q55 2012
791.43'6582—dc23
                              2011029187

Editorial Credits
Editor: Lisa Owings
Designer: Marie Tupy

Media Researcher: Emily Temple
Editorial Director: Patricia Stockland

Photo Credits
Charlie B. Ward, cover (foreground); Rob Stegmann/iStockphoto, cover (background);
Pavel Losevsky/Bigstock, cover (background); Everett Collection, 4, 15, 17; Universal/
Everett Collection, 5, 30; iStockphoto, 6; Ljupco Smokovski/Bigstock, 7; Warner Brothers/
Everett Collection, 8 (bottom), 18, 21; 20th Century Fox Film Corp./Everett Collection, 8
(top); Sony Pictures Classics/Everett Collection, 9 (top), 32; Columbia/Everett Collection,
9 (bottom); Andrey Burmakin/Dreamstime, 10; Jon Quijano/Red Line Editorial, 12;
Shutterstock Images, 14 (bottom), 40; Orange Line Media/Shutterstock Images, 14 (top);
Margie Hurwich/Shutterstock Images, 14 (center); Mary Evans/EON/Ronald Grant/Everett
Collection, 16 (top); Sergey Goruppa/Bigstock, 16 (bottom); Yuri Arcurs/Bigstock, 19;
Rick Orndorf, 20, 25, 26, 33, 34, 35 (top, middle, bottom), 36 (top, bottom), 37, 38, 39,
41 (top), 45 (top); Red Line Editorial, 22; Olga Besnard/Shutterstock Images, 23; Petro
Teslenko/Bigstock, 24; Mykola Velychko/Bigstock, 27; Menno van Dijk/iStockphoto, 28;
Humberto Ortega/Dreamstime, 29; Elemér Sági/Dreamstime, 29; Suzanne Tucker/Bigstock,
31; Jiri Hera/Bigstock, 41 (bottom); Margie Hurwich/Bigstock, 42; Kuznetsov Alexey/
Shutterstock Images, 43; Dana Rothstein/Bigstock, 45 (bottom)

Printed in the United States of America in Stevens Point, Wisconsin.
102011   006404WZS12

TABLE OF CONTENTS

INTRODUCTION TO
ACTION AND THRILLER FILMS

Your mission, should you choose to accept it, is to make your own action movie or thriller. Keep your audience on the edges of their seats with pulse-pounding chases. Throw them into the action with fierce fight scenes. Impress them with supercool special effects. Get ready for an adventure!

Action Movies vs. Thrillers

Action movies and thrillers are similar. Both rely on exciting action scenes. However, there is a key difference.

ACTION MOVIES

Action movies have confident heroes who appear unbeatable. The hero's confidence gives the audience confidence. The audience knows the good guys will beat the bad guys in the end.

Goldfinger (1964), *Braveheart* (1995), *The Lord of the Rings* (2001–2003), *Sherlock Holmes* (2009)

THRILLERS

In thrillers, heroes aren't so tough. They are more like regular people. They can be beaten in a fight. The audience feels uncertain about who will come out on top. This gives thrillers suspense.

The Bourne Identity (2002), *The Prestige* (2006), *Inception* (2010)

special effect—a visual trick used in a movie when normal techniques won't work

suspense—a prolonged feeling of tension from not knowing what will happen next

What All Action Movies Have in Common

ACTION SCENES

Action scenes, such as chase scenes or fight scenes, are fast paced. They focus on movement. Too much **dialogue** can slow down the movie. If action movie characters *do* talk, it's usually in the middle of some kind of action.

MOMENTUM

Action filmmakers create **momentum** by increasing the excitement of each scene until the movie reaches its **climax**. This keeps the audience excited and alert throughout the film.

VIOLENCE

Characters in action movies often decide that fighting is the best way to get what they want. Here are some reasons your action hero might use violence:

- Your hero has been wronged and is out for revenge.

- Someone your hero loves is in danger. The hero must fight to protect his or her loved one.

- Your hero is in the wrong place at the wrong time. He or she resorts to violence in self-defense.

- It's your hero's job to act bravely in a dangerous situation. For example, a superhero can't just stand by and watch while someone commits a violent crime.

dialogue—a conversation between two or more characters

momentum—an increase in the excitement of each scene to create a sense of forward motion

climax—the most exciting or important part of a story

ACTION HEROES

Let these action heroes inspire you as you develop your own characters.

James Bond
Casino Royale (2006)
James Bond is a charming spy who is popular with the ladies. He uses cool gadgets and drives an even cooler car.

Wolverine
X-Men (2000)
Wolverine has metal claws and the ability to heal in seconds. He is part of the superhero group the X-Men.

Maggie Fitzgerald
Million Dollar Baby (2004)
Maggie Fitzgerald is a talented boxer. She is willing to do whatever it takes to become a professional.

Lara Croft
Tomb Raider (2001)
Lara Croft is a beautiful treasure hunter with serious fighting skills.

VILLAINS

Action movie villains are bad guys that most people would avoid at all costs. But action heroes can't resist a chance to save the day. Here are some examples of common action villains:

Old Enemies
Jade Fox
Crouching Tiger, Hidden Dragon (2000)
Sometimes a villain is just someone with a grudge against your hero.

Criminals
Howard Payne
Speed (1994)
Action heroes will bravely stand up to criminals.

Spies
Major Arnold Toht
Raiders of the Lost Ark (1981)
Spies will follow your hero around and cause trouble at the worst times. They always seem to know something your hero doesn't.

Evil Geniuses
Green Goblin
Spider-Man (2002)
Evil geniuses try to gain power with brilliant plans or mega-weapons. Only an action hero can spoil their plans.

To make an action movie, you need to be organized. Drama is for the screen, not your movie shoot! You will plan every detail of your shoot during preproduction.

Create Your Plot

You need an exciting **plot** for your movie. Here are some ideas to help you brainstorm:

- Base your plot on an adventure you've been on or one a friend has told you about.

- Give a fresh twist to a classic action or thriller plot.

- Keep an eye out for news stories that have action potential, such as robberies or mysterious kidnappings. Choose one that interests you. Change or exaggerate it to make it your own.

Three-Act Structure

A good action or thriller story needs three parts: a beginning, a middle, and an end. In movies and plays, these parts are called acts.

ACT 1
- A villain causes a crisis in the opening scenes.
- The hero decides to fight the villain in the following scenes.

ACT 2
- The hero fights the villain but meets unexpected obstacles.
- The hero thinks of a plan for overcoming these obstacles.

ACT 3
- The hero follows his or her plan. The story reaches its climax during the final face-off between the hero and the villain.
- The hero either succeeds or fails in defeating the villain.

A Thrilling End

Action heroes usually succeed in defeating the villain. The ending of a thriller is harder to guess. Alfred Hitchcock's films were popular because no one knew how they would end.

plot—the main story

Write Your Script

Once you know your plot and characters, it's time to write your **script**. The script will contain all the dialogue and action that takes place in your movie.

Movie scripts follow a standard format. The font used is 12-point Courier. A film industry guideline is that each page of your script will equal about one minute of film.

CUT TO:

EXT. OVERLOOKING ENEMY JUNGLE BASE — DAY

Campfire smoke rises from the base below.

BUTCH and CID crouch in the jungle underbrush. They are looking down at the base from a hill.

Through binoculars, they see commandos in the enemy base loading large crates onto trucks.

                    BUTCH
         It will be bad news if we don't stop them from
         moving that shipment.

Butch passes the binoculars to Cid. Cid looks.

                    CID
         What do you propose we do?

                    BUTCH
                (chuckling)
         We take care of things the old-fashioned way.

Butch pats the barrel of his rocket launcher.

TIP

Before you start writing, think about how long you want your movie to be. Making movies always takes longer than you think! Most Hollywood action movies are at least 90 minutes long, but shorter films can be just as exciting.

script—the written text of a movie

- Start each scene with a heading that includes the place and time in which the scene is set. Use DAY for daytime scenes and NIGHT for evening and nighttime scenes. Use INT. (interior) or EXT. (exterior) to show whether the scene takes place indoors or outside. Make a new heading each time you move to a different place.

DESCRIPTION

- Describe the action throughout the scene in detail. What are the characters doing?
- Describe the sights and sounds in each scene. What are the characters seeing, hearing, and reacting to?

DIALOGUE

- Show who is speaking by writing the speaker's name in capital letters above each character's line.
- Write your characters' dialogue. Keep it simple and to the point. It is usually best to let your actors decide how to deliver their lines. However, you can include instructions in parentheses if needed.

Breaking Down Your Script

Most movies are shot out of order. All scenes that take place in the same location are shot at once. To stay organized, do what professional filmmakers do and break down your script. Go through your completed script. Make a list of where and when each scene needs to be shot. Also list the characters and props you need for each scene. Group together all scenes that need to be shot in the same place and at the same time. Use your list to make a shoot schedule. If you need to shoot outside, have a backup plan in case of bad weather.

Shooting Locations

Where will your story take place? Easy options will be your home, your school, and public areas such as parks or neighborhood streets. Always ask permission before shooting in any location.

A school or office building is a good setting for your characters' secret operations.

Your basement, attic, or garage may work for a hero's or villain's hideout.

An old neighborhood with narrow alleys will work well for a foot chase.

Set Pieces

Action movies are built on long, elaborate action scenes called set pieces. Set pieces often move the story in a new direction or reveal something about a character. A set piece involving a daring rescue might show how much the hero cares about another character.

In the first set piece of *Raiders of the Lost Ark* (1981), Indiana Jones escapes a booby-trapped shrine with a golden statue. Then he loses the statue to his rival, Belloq.

TIP

Many action filmmakers think of set pieces first and create a story to connect them afterward. Come up with set pieces that fit your resources. Be sure you can realistically shoot all the important elements.

Storyboarding

Storyboards are important for planning your shoots. Storyboard your action scenes by making a sketch of each planned shot. When filming, storyboards help you remember all the shots you need. When editing, they help you remember the order of the shots.

storyboard for *Tomorrow Never Dies* (1997)

LOW ANGLE TRACKING BEHIND PURSUIT CAR IN STREET.

Cast and Crew

As the director of an action movie, you will need to find your cast and crew. Ask your friends and relatives if they would like to help make your movie. Seek out people who are experienced in martial arts, gymnastics, parkour, or other sports. You could also hold auditions. You could even play a few roles yourself!

Seven Samurai (1954)

Seven Samurai is a samurai flick. It is about a team of samurai who protect a village from bandits. *Seven Samurai* was one of the first action movies. Many action movies today still copy its methods of introducing characters.

The Stand-Alone Opening

Many action movies introduce the hero with an adventure that is not part of the main story. The first scene in *Seven Samurai* introduces the samurai Kambe. He rescues a child from a thief. It is a quick, exciting way to show his bravery.

Building a Team

Spend time introducing each of your characters. Brief action scenes in *Seven Samurai* highlight the strengths of each samurai.

parkour—the sport of navigating obstacles in the landscape by running, climbing, or jumping

samurai—special class of warriors who fought for local lords in ancient Japan

Samurai Flick Features

- samurai warriors
- sword fights with samurai swords
- historical costumes and settings
- the samurai code, *bushido*, stressing military skill, honor, and loyalty

Ocean's Eleven (2001)

Ocean's *Eleven* is a **heist** movie. A heist movie is a type of thriller. These movies focus on a team of criminals who plan a difficult robbery. Heist movies are exciting to watch because the robbery could go wrong at any moment.

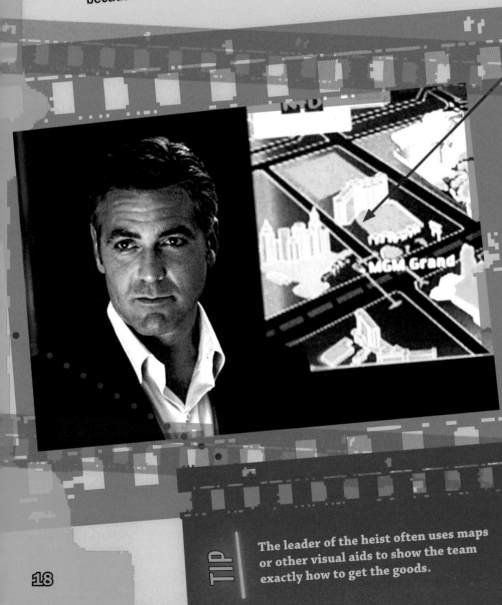

TIP

The leader of the heist often uses maps or other visual aids to show the team exactly how to get the goods.

Building the Team

A heist movie often begins with the leader building a team to help with the robbery. In *Ocean's Eleven*, Danny Ocean needs the help of 11 people with unique talents to rob three major Las Vegas casinos.

Revealing the Plan

The audience needs to know how the team plans to do the heist without getting caught. The leader of the heist carefully describes the plan to the rest of the team.

Plot Twists

The most exciting heists never go as planned. The *Ocean's Eleven* team gets caught in the act. They are forced to come up with a creative solution to escape with the cash.

Disguises

Robbers often wear sneaky disguises. Good costumes will help make your movie memorable.

heist—a robbery

Costumes

Look for costumes in the following places:

- army surplus stores
- martial arts supply stores
- costume shops/uniform shops
- thrift stores/consignment shops

ACT 2:
LIGHTS, CAMERA, ACTION!

The production phase of the shoot is where the real action begins. You will shoot all of the scenes for your movie during production.

Directing a Set Piece

Rehearsal

Before you begin shooting a set piece, spend a day rehearsing it. Have your actors perform their movements until they are comfortable with their parts. Calmly discuss any problems that come up. Work with your actors to find solutions.

Filming

1. Gather your cast and crew. Review the storyboards of the shots you have planned for the day.

2. Have your crew help you set up each shot with the correct props, equipment, and lighting.

3. Review each shot with the actors. Give them positive feedback throughout the shoot. Frame any negative feedback as polite suggestions.

4. Use your storyboards to make sure you get every shot you need. When you are done filming, thank your cast and crew for their help. Let them know they did a great job.

Cinematography

Action and thriller filmmakers use cinematography to heighten the sense of movement and excitement. Cinematography is the art of movie photography. It includes how shots and scenes are put together, camera angle and placement, lighting, and special effects.

300 (2006)

Three-Point Lighting

Classic Hollywood lighting uses three lights. Three-point lighting creates bright light with few shadows. An evenly lit scene adds to the confident mood of action movies. It also helps the audience see the details of the action.

1. The Key Light

The key light is the main light on your subject. It is the brightest light, and it casts the darkest shadows.

2. The Fill Light

The fill light is a secondary light. It lightens the shadows created by the key light.

3. The Back Light

The back light shines from behind your subject. It helps set your actor apart from the background.

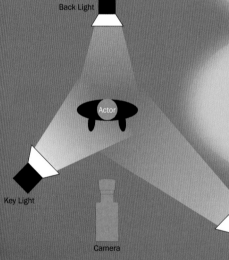

Back Light

Actor

Key Light

Camera

Fill Light

TIP

Stage lights are available for rent but can get dangerously hot. Always wear heavy cloth or leather gloves when handling them.

The Art of Shadows

Use lighting to help create suspense in your thriller. Here are some lighting techniques to try:

- Lose the fill light. Use only the key light and back light. This will create dark shadows on your actors. This technique works well to make villains look even scarier.

- Shine the key light from below your subject. Shining the key light up at an actor from below creates a spooky effect. Use this lighting to create a feeling of danger or suspense.

- Take a shot in the dark. Shooting at night or in a dimly lit room is another way to create suspense in your thriller. Who knows what could be lurking in the shadows?

Finding Lights to Use

Try using the lamps in your house to light your scene. House lamps with swivel necks are best because you can aim the light. Put the same type of bulb in every lamp so your light has an even tone.

Camera Movement

The most important part of action movies is movement. Use camera movement to enhance the on-screen action.

Tracking Shot

A tracking shot lets your audience follow the action while the shot stays smooth and stable. Traditional tracking shots use wheels to keep the camera from shaking as it rolls along a track. However, you can get a tracking shot without fancy equipment.

Wheelchair Tracking Shot

1. The cameraperson sits in the wheelchair.
2. A second person pushes the wheelchair, following the actors as the cameraperson films.

If You Don't Have a Wheelchair

You can use any type of cart of dolly that rolls smoothly and quietly for a tracking shot. Try tying your camera to a skateboard. Push the skateboard behind your actors to get a shot of just their feet moving.

pan—to turn the camera to the left or right while filming

Whip Pan

Whip **pans** are camera movements that quickly move the camera from one subject to another. Whip pans are often used in fight scenes. Use these quick camera movements to add to the on-screen motion.

1. Start filming one actor or object.
2. Using a quick, smooth motion, pan the camera to focus on something else.

Finding a Camera

You can make a great action movie with any camera. It should be easy to find a family video camera or a still camera that takes video. You can also rent a higher-quality camera.

Practical Effects

Practical effects are special effects performed live for the camera during production.

FAKE EXPLOSION

You will need:

wooden board about 2 inches (5 cm) thick, 6 inches (15 cm) wide, and 2 feet (0.6 m) long

flour

1. Lay the board over an uneven spot on the ground. A curb works well. The board should function as a seesaw. About three-fourths of the board should rest on the ground. The rest of the board should rest on the curb.

2. Dump a pile of flour on the end of the board that is touching the ground.

3. Use a bush, trash can, or other prop to hide the board from the camera's view.

4. Have the actor run past and stomp on the raised end of the board. This action will catapult the flour into the air. From a distance, the flour looks like an explosion.

WALL RUN

You will need:

wall   **chair**

1. Film your actor running toward the wall. Have your actor jump as though about to run up the wall.

2. Set the chair next to the wall. Have your actor sit on the chair with his or her feet touching the wall. Film your actor's feet "running" a few steps along the wall.

3. Film your actor jumping down from the wall.

4. Later, you will edit these shots together to make a continuous scene.

Chroma-Keying

Many action films use chroma-keying. The action is filmed against a green background called a green screen. Later, a computer program replaces the green background with a new background.

MAKE YOUR OWN GREEN SCREEN

You will need:

thumbtacks or tape

an 8- by 12-foot (2.4- by 3.7-m) piece of bright green, non-reflective fabric

Chroma Keys

Nothing you want in your green screen shot can be green, because chroma-keying will remove it along with the background.

Position objects and actors far enough from the screen so that they don't cast shadows on it. Shadows make chroma-keying difficult.

1. Iron your fabric if it is wrinkled or creased.

2. Use the thumbtacks or tape to hang your green screen on a wall.

Optional: If you have more money to spend, you can buy special green screen material or a premade green screen. Look for these on the Internet.

Drive a Car Off a Cliff

You will need:

- video camera
- tripod
- large cardboard box painted bright green
- green screen
- realistic model car
- chroma-keying software (often included in a standard video editing program)

1. With your camera on a tripod, film the edge of a cliff. Film for at least twice as long as your shot will be.

2. Place the cardboard box in front of the green screen. One edge of the cardboard box will represent the edge of the cliff.

3. Light the green screen and box evenly. Get rid of any shadows.

4. Place the model car on top of the box. Light the car from the same position as the sun in your cliff shot.

5. With your camera on a tripod, begin filming. Push the car off the box. Get a good shot of the car flying through the air. Make sure your hand is never in the shot.

6. Load the green screen shot into your chroma-keying software. Use the software to replace the background.

Screening Room

The Bourne Identity (2002)

The Bourne Identity is a chase movie. A chase movie is a type of thriller. In chase movies, the hero spends the entire movie running from an enemy. Jason Bourne's adventures include a cool car chase through the streets of Paris.

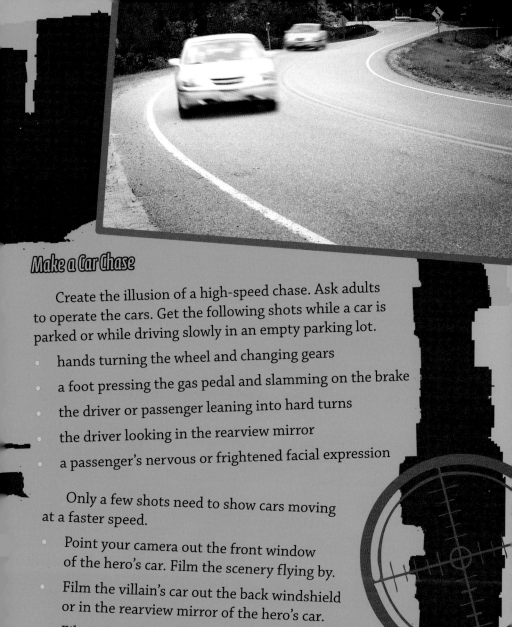

Make a Car Chase

Create the illusion of a high-speed chase. Ask adults to operate the cars. Get the following shots while a car is parked or while driving slowly in an empty parking lot.

- hands turning the wheel and changing gears
- a foot pressing the gas pedal and slamming on the brake
- the driver or passenger leaning into hard turns
- the driver looking in the rearview mirror
- a passenger's nervous or frightened facial expression

Only a few shots need to show cars moving at a faster speed.

- Point your camera out the front window of the hero's car. Film the scenery flying by.
- Film the villain's car out the back windshield or in the rearview mirror of the hero's car.
- Film a few shots of the cars driving past you in different locations. Film them turning corners too.

TIP

Later you can add sound effects of revving engines and squealing tires to make it sound like the cars are going very fast.

Crouching Tiger, Hidden Dragon (2002)

Crouching Tiger, Hidden Dragon is a type of action movie called a kung fu movie. Kung fu movies are built around martial arts fight scenes. *Crouching Tiger, Hidden Dragon* is known for its acrobatic fight scenes.

Make a Fight Scene

- Draw each move in a sequence of storyboards.
- Set your fight moves to a repeating count of four, like a dance. This will help your actors memorize the fight sequence.

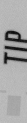
How to Fake a Punch

1. The punching hand should move in a side-to-side motion across the opponent's face, at least 1 foot (0.3 m) away from the opponent's face.

2. Have the opponent snap his or her head back with a look of pain in reaction to the punch.

3. Film from behind the puncher. The camera angle will make the punch look real.

4. Use editing software to add a punch sound effect at the point of impact.

kung fu—a type of Chinese martial art similar to karate that is used for self-defense; kung fu uses blocks, kicks, and punches

choreography—the creation and arrangement of a sequence of movements

Shoot for Editing

When you are filming, try to get all of the following shots. They are the building blocks you will use to create a scene.

ESTABLISHING SHOT

An establishing shot shows where the scene is taking place. Use it at the beginning of a scene.

MASTER SHOT

A master shot shows the actors performing the entire scene. Show as much of the master shot as you want. Cut to close-ups to show details such as facial expressions.

MEDIUM SHOTS AND CLOSE-UPS

Get a variety of shots of all your actors during each scene. A close-up brings special attention to a specific detail in a scene.

Medium Shot (MS): shows the actor from above the knee

Close-Up (CU): shows a detail from the scene up close

Extreme Close-Up (XCU): shows only a small part of an actor or object in the scene

Reaction Shots

Show each actor's response to other actors or events.

TIP

You may not get another chance to shoot a scene, so do a few takes of every shot.

Insert Shots

Get close-ups of important details in the scene, such as a bomb about to go off or a piece of evidence that proves your villain guilty.

take—footage from one continuous camera run

ACT 3:
AFTER THE SHOOT

Congratulations! You've finished your shoot. Now it's time to edit what you shot into a movie. The editing part of the project is called postproduction.

Editing

You will use video editing software to edit your movie. Most computers come with basic video editing software. Computer stores sell more advanced editing software, but it can be expensive. The quality of the software is less important than your creativity in using it.

Action Film Editing

As an action filmmaker, you want your story to move quickly. Editing gives you power over the movie's pace. Edit your scenes to leave out anything that slows down your scene unnecessarily.

In a slow-paced movie, a scene might stretch over many shots.

To speed up the scene for an action movie, only these shots would remain.

Action Movie Sound

Sound is a special challenge in action movies. Action scenes are known for having big explosions, roaring car engines, and other loud sounds. You will add most of these sound effects to the movie after the shoot.

FOLEY

Sound effects added during editing are called Foley. With just a microphone, a quiet room, and a little creativity, you can record Foley for your action movie. Try the following examples. Then see if you can come up with your own!

Gun Shot

Fire a cap gun.

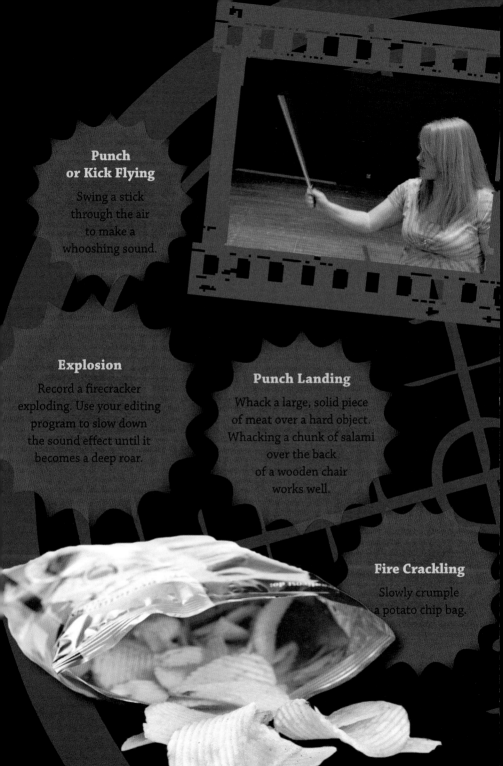

Punch or Kick Flying

Swing a stick through the air to make a whooshing sound.

Explosion

Record a firecracker exploding. Use your editing program to slow down the sound effect until it becomes a deep roar.

Punch Landing

Whack a large, solid piece of meat over a hard object. Whacking a chunk of salami over the back of a wooden chair works well.

Fire Crackling

Slowly crumple a potato chip bag.

Music

Add excitement to your gripping action scenes with movie music, called a score. Many action heroes have a musical theme. Indiana Jones performs each of his daring deeds to the same upbeat tune. Spooky or fast-paced music can create suspense. Match the music to the mood of each scene.

WHERE TO GET YOUR SCORE

- Buy prerecorded music online.
- Write and record the music yourself.
- Have a friend or relative write and record music for you.

Visual Effects

Visual effects are special effects often created during postproduction. You can use your video editing software to create visual effects. Your software's manual, help function, or online tutorials will tell you what effects you can create and how to create them. You can learn how to add explosions, flames, flying debris, lightning flashes, laser beams, and more to your movie.

EPILOGUE:
YOUR PREMIERE

Mission accomplished! You set out to make a heart-racing action movie, and you did it. You came up with a slick script, and then you brought your vision to life. Now all you need is an audience!

Many small movie theaters let you rent their screens for showings. Your local school or library also might have an auditorium for your premiere date.

How to Make Your Premiere a Success

1. One month before your premiere date, send invitations to your family, friends, and everyone who helped make your movie.

2. Plan a short speech introducing your movie and thanking your team.

3. Serve refreshments and snacks after the movie. Be prepared to answer questions.

4. Give your audience response cards to fill out. Ask them what they liked and didn't like about your movie. You may be able to use their feedback to improve films you make in the future.

TIP

You can have your premiere at home too! If you have a projector and projection screen, set them up in your living room. Otherwise, your TV will work just fine.

Give Your Premiere an Action-Packed Theme

In a tin or plastic container, give your guests "survival kits" that reflect your movie's theme. Here are some ideas:

- Snacks that fit your film. For example, a scene in *Raiders of the Lost Ark* had fruits called dates. If this were your movie, you could include a few dates in your kits.

- A "treasure map" of your premiere site or a mock news article about your hero or villain.

- Some small gift, such as a magnifying glass, plastic compass, or other gadget.

Decorate your premiere site to match your movie's theme. You could even set up props from your movie outside the screening room.

Play action-packed music before and after the movie. Include music from your film's score.

GLOSSARY

choreography (kor-ee-AH-gruh-fee)—the creation and arrangement of a sequence of movements

climax (KLYE-maks)—the most exciting or important part of a story

dialogue (DYE-uh-lawg)—a conversation between two or more characters

heist (HYST)—a robbery

kung fu (KUHNG FOO)—a type of Chinese martial art similar to karate that is used for self-defense; kung fu uses blocks, kicks, and punches

momentum (moh-MEN-tuhm)—an increase in the excitement of each scene to create a sense of forward motion

pan (PAN)—to turn the camera to the left or right while filming

parkour (pahr-KOOR)—the sport of navigating obstacles in the landscape by running, climbing, or jumping

plot (PLAHT)—the main story

samurai (SAM-uh-rye)—a special class of warriors who fought for local lords in ancient Japan

script (SKRIPT)—the written text of a movie

special effect (SPESH-uhl i-FEKT)—a visual trick used in a movie when normal techniques won't work

suspense (suh-SPENS)—a prolonged feeling of tension from not knowing what will happen next

take (TAYK)—footage from one continuous camera run

READ MORE

Grabham, Tim, et. al. *Movie Maker*. Somerville, Mass.: Candlewick Press, 2010.

Lanier, Troy, and Clay Nichols. *Filmmaking for Teens: Pulling Off Your Shorts*. Studio City, Cal.: Michael Weise Productions, 2010.

Miles, Liz. *Movie Special Effects*. Culture in Action. Chicago: Raintree, 2010.

Thomas, William. *Movie Stunt Worker*. Dirty and Dangerous Jobs. New York: Marshall Cavendish Benchmark, 2010.

INTERNET SITES

FactHound offers a safe, fun way to find Internet sites related to this book. All of the sites on FactHound have been researched by our staff.

Here's all you do:

Visit *www.facthound.com*

Type in this code: 9781429675291

INDEX